Giant Leaps

The Gemini Spacewalkers

Stuart A. Kallen

ABDO & Daughters
PUBLISHING

Published by Abdo & Daughters, 4940 Viking Dr., Suite 622, Edina, MN 55435.

Cover Photos by: Archive Photos, Bettmann
Inside Photos by:
Archive Photos: pp. 7, 16, 21, 28
AP/Wide World Photos: pp. 7, 11, 14, 24, 25
Bettmann: pp. 4, 8, 13, 15, 17, 19, 23, 27

Edited by Bob Italia

Library of Congress Cataloging–in–Publication Data

Kallen, Stuart A., 1955–
The Gemini spacewalkers / Stuart A. Kallen
    p. cm. — (Giant leaps)
Includes bibliographical references (p. 31) and index.
Summary: Discusses Project Gemini's two unmanned and ten manned missions; spacewalking, the spacewalkers, and their Soviet counterparts; and moving on to Project Apollo and the moon.
ISBN 1-56239-567-X
1. Project Gemini (U.S.)—Juvenile literature. 2. Extravehicular activity (Manned space flight)—Juvenile literature. [1. Project Gemini. 2. Extravehicular activity (Manned space flight) 3. Space flight.] I. Title. II. Series.
TL789.8.U6G399   1996
629.45'4—dc20   95-40476
                                                               CIP
                                                               AC

CONTENTS

THE STORY OF PROJECT GEMINI

FOR THOUSANDS OF YEARS human beings have gazed into the night skies. Ancient stargazers saw scorpions, lions, fish, and other creatures in the shapes of the stars, and called them constellations. Constellations also took on human names—the Seven Sisters, the Herdsman, and the Painter.

Perhaps the most fascinating constellation is Gemini—Latin for "twins." The ancient Greeks who named Gemini could not imagine a day when two people could travel into outer space together. But thousands of years after Gemini's discovery, Project Gemini took on a life of its own.

The year was 1963. The United States and the Soviet Union—two of the most powerful countries on earth were locked in a battle to land a man on the moon. Each country had hundreds of nuclear missiles pointed at the other. They strived for loyalty from all other countries. No one knew if or when those missiles might be launched. It was a standoff. It frightened millions of people. This era was called the Cold War. It began in 1945 and lasted until the Communist government of the Soviet Union collapsed in 1991. It was a war fought with images on television and words written in newspapers. It was fought in countries like Korea and Vietnam. And it was fought in a race to the moon.

The Soviets had been first to put a man in space in 1957. The United States quickly followed. For the next eight years each country tried to outdo the other. Flights became longer. Difficult maneuvers were executed. Every year another space record was set, then shattered.

Of course, the race to space was more than a bitter fight. People in both countries took pride in their scientists and astronauts. Millions of people watched TV coverage whenever a spacecraft was launched. The astronauts were real heroes whose skill and bravery satisfied that basic human urge—to go farther, reach higher, and go where no one has ever gone before.

This page: Gemini 6 and Gemini 7 prepare to dock in space.

PROJECT GEMINI

The first Americans in space were part of Project Mercury, named after the Greek god with wings on his feet. A Mercury capsule first put astronaut Alan Shepard into sub-orbital flight on May 5, 1961. Lieutenant Major John Glenn was the first American to orbit the earth on February 20, 1962. His Mercury capsule was called *Friendship 7*. On May 15 and 16, 1963, an American astronaut, L. Gordon Cooper, Jr., orbited the earth 22 times in a spacecraft he named the *Faith 7*. This was the last of six successful Project Mercury flights. The research and knowledge gathered from the Mercury flights was put to use in Project Gemini.

The long-range goal was to put a man on the moon. The plans were already on the drawing boards at the National Aeronautics and Space Administration—NASA—America's space agency. The moon project would be called Apollo. The Lunar Module (LM) to land on the moon would contain over one million parts packed into a craft the size of a delivery van. NASA planned to work on the Gemini and Apollo projects at the same time.

Much more information on spaceflight was needed before a moon landing could be attempted. Two spacecraft had to meet in outer space and join together. Space suits had to protect astronauts from the vacuum and radiation of space. The suits would be tested during space walks. Two-man spaceflights had to be attempted. Project Gemini would be a proving ground for Project Apollo's moon landing, still years in the future. Across America, university think tanks and aerospace companies geared up for the challenge.

Top Right: Astronauts Michael Collins and John Young in the *Gemini 10* spacecraft.

Right: A cutaway view showing the insides of the Gemini spacecraft, compared to the earlier Mercury capsule.

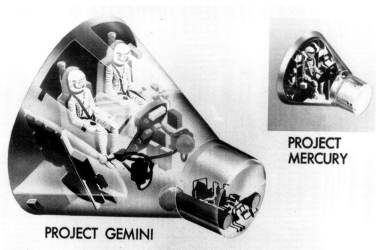

PROJECT GEMINI

PROJECT
MERCURY

SOVIET RECORD BREAKERS

The Soviet Union had matched or beaten every American achievement in space. In 1962, the Soviets launched the first "group flight" of two spacecraft orbiting at the same time. These capsules were called *Vostok 3* and *Vostok 4*. The Vostok (Hawk) capsules had flown within 4 miles (6.5 kilometers) of each other. A Vostok pilot (called a *cosmonaut*) even took live TV pictures that were beamed back to earth.

In 1963, the Soviets did it again. They arranged another group flight—but this time with a twist. Cosmonaut Valery Bykovsky was launched aboard *Vostok 5* on June 14. Two days later, Valentina V. Tereshkova was launched aboard *Vostok 6*. She was the first woman to fly into space. The two capsules did not orbit together. In fact, they were thousands of miles apart. But Tereshkova, a factory worker who was also a parachute jumper, entered the record books as the first woman in space.

The next Soviet flight sent three men into orbit. This mission was called Voskhod (Ruby). Because the capsule was so small, the men could not wear space suits to protect them in an emergency. Luckily, the flight went smoothly, and the three men returned to earth safely. It was a risk, but the Soviets had put three men in flight at once.

Left: Cosmonaut Valentina V. Tereshkova.

BIGGER AND BETTER GEMINI

At NASA, little attention was given to the Vostok and Voskhod launches. There were thousands of projects to finish if a man was to walk on the moon by 1970.

The Gemini capsule was built. It looked like a bigger version of the Mercury capsule. It had the same shape—an upside-down badminton "birdie." The outside was covered with rippled metal shingles. The capsule's wide bottom was covered with a heat shield. It would protect Gemini from the white-hot temperatures generated during reentry into earth's atmosphere.

But there were differences between Mercury and Gemini capsules. Experience had shown that equipment could be placed in another module outside the pressurized cabin. The module could be left behind during reentry.

Another change allowed Gemini's rockets to move the capsule to different altitudes during orbit.

This provided pin-point landings. Gemini used a fuel-cell system that combined liquid hydrogen with oxygen to make fresh drinking water and electricity. (Astronauts said the water tasted terrible.) Gemini's nose cone was designed to lock onto—or dock—with another space vehicle. The Gemini capsule was over 18 feet (5.5 meters) long and over 7 feet (2 meters) wide. The capsule weighed almost 8,300 pounds (3,765 kilograms).

The Gemini capsule sat on top of a huge rocket that would carry it into space. The rocket was an intercontinental ballistic missile (ICBM) called the Titan II. It was also used by the Air Force to carry nuclear warheads—to the Soviet Union if necessary. The Titan had made over 100 successful launches. NASA launched two successful flights of unmanned Gemini spacecraft. The missions proved Gemini ready for manned flights.

SOVIET SPACEWALKERS

The head of the Soviet space program, Sergei Korolev, heard about the Gemini project. He wanted a Soviet cosmonaut to be the first person to walk in space. Using dangerous and unproven equipment, Korolev launched *Voskhod 2*. It was March 8, 1965—five days before Gemini's first manned flight. The first man to walk in space would be Cosmonaut Aleksey Leonov.

With some difficulty, Leonov left the capsule and floated through space in front of a TV camera mounted on the capsule. After nine minutes, Leonov was ordered back into the capsule. But his space suit had swollen during his brief spacewalk. Leonov could not even bend to enter the hatch. He pulled as hard as he could. His racing heart and rapid breathing quickly drained the oxygen supply strapped on his back. Leonov risked his life by reducing the pressure in his suit. After a frightening eight minutes he slid back into the capsule.

But Leonov's troubles were not over. The automatic retrorockets that were supposed to push the capsule back into the atmosphere did not work. Leonov fired them by hand. The capsule hurled toward earth, 1,300 miles (2,091 kilometers) off course. Leonov landed in a snowbound mountain forest in the northern Soviet Union. The capsule was half buried in the snow. The cosmonaut waited all day for a rescue helicopter. When it got dark, the frozen Leonov built a fire to warm himself and to scare away wolves that were circling. Finally ski troops rescued Leonov the next morning.

Although the mission was a near disaster, American newspapers, radios, and televisions blared the news of Leonov's spacewalk. They said that Soviet technology was better than America's. The Soviets did not reveal the mistakes and life-threatening dangers until 20 years later. They had scored another victory in the American media.

Right: Cosmonaut Aleksey Leonov. *Inset:* Leonov on his historic spacewalk.

SPACEWALKER WHITE

On the morning of March 23, 1965, Commander Gus Grissom, along with Navy pilot Lieutenant Commander John Young, slid through the twin hatchways into the cramped *Gemini 3* spacecraft. This was not Grissom's first launch. He had made a sub-orbital flight in a Mercury capsule in 1961. After that flight, he had almost drown when the hatchway blew out and the capsule sank after splashdown in the ocean.

The massive Titan rocket stood over 130 feet (40 meters) high. The launch was perfect. The spacecraft behaved well. The two men completed a series of biological and radiation experiments. The cramped cabin was very small, even in the weightlessness of space. Grissom unwrapped a corned beef sandwich that he had smuggled on board the ship. He quickly put it away when pink crumbs of meat began floating around the capsule. During landing, one of the three parachutes did not open properly. Both astronauts were violently flung into the capsule's windows, breaking the faceplate on Grissom's helmet.

Remembering how he almost drown in the Mercury capsule, Grissom would not open the hatchway after splashdown. It took 30 minutes for Navy frogmen to rescue the seasick astronauts from the hot cabin pitching on the ocean waves. But the flight had proven that the Gemini capsule was "spaceworthy." Grissom was severely scolded for the corned beef sandwich incident. The food crumbs could have shorted out important equipment in the capsule.

Gemini 4 was launched on June 3, 1965. Captain Edward White flew as pilot and Captain James McDivitt flew as mission commander. Both men were from the Air Force. This was the first Gemini flight to include a spacewalk.

Right: Gemini liftoff.

Once again the launch was flawless. Television coverage of the blastoff was broadcast to Europe using the new Early Bird satellite. Besides putting men in orbit, the United States had been launching television, radio, and telephone satellites. This began a revolution in communications that is still in progress today.

To prepare for the spacewalk, Ed White went through some very tiring exercises. He had to attach a line from the capsule to the space suit. He then had to attach his emergency oxygen pack to his chest pack in the tiny cockpit. After resting, White opened the hatch while the spacecraft was over the Indian Ocean. He stood up and fired a hand-held "zip" gun that squirted compressed gas. This thrust White out of the capsule and into space. White could see the Pacific below him and the bright sun above him. He floated on the end of his tether. After 15 minutes, McDivitt told White to reel himself in and close the hatch. White did not want to leave free-floating space. "It's the saddest moment of my life," he said as he pulled himself back in.

Like Leonov, White had a hard time fitting the bulky suit through the narrow hatch. It was even harder to operate the handle to reseal the spacecraft. But with McDivitt's help, *Gemini 4* was repressurized. Next came the tiring task of putting away the spacewalking equipment. The picture of Ed White floating free, thruster gun in his right hand, with distant clouds reflected in his mirrored visor became the most famous picture of the time.

Left: Astronaut Ed White, America's first spacewalker, tethered to the orbiting *Gemini 4* spacecraft.

Right: White takes his first step into space.

RENDEZVOUS IN ORBIT

Less than three months after *Gemini 4*, *Gemini 5* was launched. It was an eight-day mission. The capsule was stocked with a new product—spacefood, squeezed out of tubes. L. Gordon Cooper—who had flown the last Mercury mission—

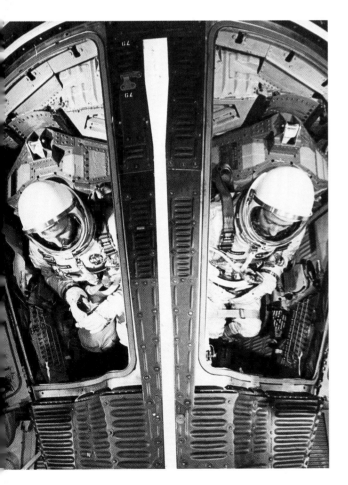

would be the commander. Navy Lieutenant Charles "Pete" Conrad would be the pilot. The mission's purpose was to practice docking with another spacecraft. NASA called it a rendezvous (RAHN-day-voo), the French word for "meeting." Since no other craft was ready, the astronauts would practice reaching a certain point in space. *Gemini 5* was a perfect flight marred only by a computer error upon landing. The capsule overshot its target by 80 miles (129 kilometers). It was an error, but not a dangerous one. Gordon Cooper had become the first American to fly two orbital spaceflights.

Left: Astronauts James A. McDivitt and Edward H. White inside the *Gemini 4* spacecraft.

Right: Gemini 6 maneuvered to within a few feet of *Gemini 7* to accomplish the world's first rendezvous in space on December 15, 1965.

The Gemini program made spaceflight seem simple and easy. NASA had been launching and landing picture-perfect missions.

Gemini 6 would be the first space rendezvous where two spacecraft would move very close to each other. Commander Wally Schirra and Captain Tom Stafford would lock onto an unmanned satellite—named Agena—while in orbit.

On October 25, 1965, *Gemini 6* stood ready to launch. A half mile (.80 kilometers) away, the gleaming Atlas-Agena roared to life and climbed through the sky over Cape Canaveral. Gemini would launch in a few minutes. But the Agena's engines malfunctioned. The tiny target satellite broke up. Millions of dollars in technology turned into smoking cinders that rained down on the Florida coast. The *Gemini 6* countdown was canceled.

NASA decided that *Gemini 7* would dock with *Gemini 6*. *Gemini 7* was quickly readied. On December 4, NASA launched *Gemini 7* with Air Force Major Frank Borman and Navy Lieutenant Commander James A. Lovell. They had enough food and water to last 14 days.

Gemini 6 was launched on December 15. The two astronauts aboard the *Gemini 7* spacecraft performed medical and other scientific experiments while waiting for *Gemini 6*. In order to make life more comfortable for two weeks in space, the astronauts were fitted with new lightweight space suits.

Once in orbit, *Gemini 6* found itself 1,238 miles (1,992 kilometers) behind *Gemini 7*. After three hours the distance had shrunk to 270 miles (434 kilometers). At a distance of 62 miles (100 kilometers) Schirra thought he saw the constellation Sirius. But it was *Gemini 7*. To celebrate, Wally Schirra played "Jingle Bells" on a harmonica he had brought aboard.

Soon the two spacecraft were only 131 feet (40 meters) apart. The two craft orbited around the earth two times, sometimes closing within 1 foot (.3 meters) of each other. The next day, *Gemini 6* executed a controlled reentry into the earth's atmosphere, landing only 8 miles (13 kilometers) from its target.

Gemini 7 had three days to go. The astronauts were tired after the excitement of the rendezvous. The men drifted silently, reading books they had brought along. On December 18, *Gemini 7* returned to earth 7 miles (11 kilometers) from

their target. They had spent almost 14 days in space—330 hours, 35 minutes. The weary astronauts had circled the earth 206 times. NASA had proved that men could survive in space long enough for a round trip to the moon.

Above: The *Gemini 7* spacecraft soars high above the earth during its historic rendezvous with *Gemini 6* on December 15, 1965.

WALKING AND DOCKING FAILURES

Gemini 8 was launched on March 16, 1966. Inside were civilian test pilot Neil Armstrong and Air Force Captain David R. Scott. Neil Armstrong would later be the first person to walk on the moon. But during that week in March, *Gemini 8* almost became America's first space tragedy.

The launch of *Gemini 8* went smoothly. Soon the spacecraft caught up with the Agena satellite that had been launched 101 minutes before. After floating near Agena for an hour, Mission Control told the astronauts to dock. The spacecraft's neck eased into the open throat of Agena's docking adapter. Mechanical latches sprang out to connect the two vehicles.

"We're docked," Armstrong called out. "It's a real smoothie."

People in Mission Control erupted in cheers. Successful orbital docking brought NASA one step closer to landing on the moon. With the docking technology, a moon Landing Module (LM) could fly astronauts to the moon and return them to a space capsule for the trip back to earth.

The cheering stopped when the Gemini-Agena began a slow roll. Soon the two vehicles were spinning out of control. If the roll became too violent, it would damage the neck of *Gemini 8* where the landing parachutes were stored. Then the astronauts could not return to earth.

"We have serious problems here," called Scott. "We're tumbling end over end."

One of *Gemini 8's* retrorockets would not shut off. This spun the capsule one revolution per second. The astronauts could not focus on the instrument panel, their vision blurred, and they became dizzy. Armstrong finally stopped the roll by shutting down the spacecraft's maneuvering systems. They fired emergency retrorockets over the African Congo, then began their rapid descent into the atmosphere. For 15 minutes they stared out the window hoping to see

the Pacific Ocean. They were afraid they might land in a jungle.

Gemini 8 finally opened its parachute 200 miles (321 kilometers) southeast of Japan. A search aircraft spotted them and dropped rescue frogmen.

After splashdown, the frogmen struggled to attach a flotation device to the capsule. Fifteen-foot (4.6 meter) waves tossed the capsule like a toy. After two hours, the seasick astronauts finally climbed aboard the destroyer *Mason*.

Above: The Agena Target Docking Vehicle as seen from *Gemini 8*.

If a moon flight were to be successful, then docking would have to be perfected. The first attempt was a disaster. There was no cheering that day at Mission Control.

The bad luck and technical failures that troubled *Gemini 8* continued with *Gemini 9*. The spacecraft was launched on June 3, 1966, with Navy Lieutenant Eugene A. Cernan and Thomas P. Stafford aboard. *Gemini 9* was to rendezvous and dock with an Agena satellite. However, the Agena became lost in space. The mission was changed so that *Gemini 9* would dock with an unmanned spacecraft called the Augmented Target Docking Adapter (ATDA).

The launch went smoothly and *Gemini 9* soon met with the ATDA in outer space. As Stafford fired the thrusters to bring the Gemini capsule alongside the ATDA, he saw a big problem. A wire that had held a tarp over the satellite before launch had not been removed. The multimillion-dollar mission was now in jeopardy because of a 50-cent piece of wire. Cernan was supposed to take a spacewalk after docking. Now, the spacewalk would have to be put on hold because the wire might puncture his space suit. *Gemini 9* drifted away from the ATDA.

Two days later, Cernan began his walk in space. He was supposed to leave the cabin in a bulky space suit and float free in space. But Cernan could not operate his space suit properly. His smallest movements sent him tumbling out on the end of his lifeline. His air tubes whipped around him. He was totally exhausted. All the hard work fogged his helmet visor, making it impossible to see. The spacewalk was canceled. Both *Gemini 9* missions ended in failure. The spacecraft returned to earth after its 45th orbit. It safely landed only 3,000 feet (914 meters) from its target.

Right: The Agena Target Docking Vehicle after its tether has been jettisoned from the *Gemini 11* spacecraft.

SUCCESS AT LAST

Gemini 10 would face the toughest mission so far. It was to rendezvous with two separate satellites in two different orbits. The *Gemini 10* would dock with an Agena capsule, then the two capsules would rendezvous with the Agena 8 capsule that had been left in space after the disastrous *Gemini 8* mission. There was also to be a spacewalk. *Gemini 10* would be the first mission to try all the maneuvers needed for a moon landing.

On July 18, Air Force pilot John W. Young and Captain Michael Collins climbed aboard the Gemini capsule. After six hours they moved into position to dock with an Agena capsule that had been launched 90 minutes earlier. This time the docking was successful. By firing thrusters, the twin capsules soared high into space for a rendezvous with the *Agena 8*. The twin capsules floated through space for 39 hours, only 11 miles (18 kilometers) from the *Agena 8*. Then the crew backed away from the first Agena capsule.

Collins prepared for his walk in space. The capsule moved towards the *Agena 8*. Two hours later, Collins left the spacecraft and floated up to *Agena 8*. He removed an experiment that had been left on it and returned to Gemini.

The crew did more scientific experiments before returning safely to earth. The mission had been a success.

Left: Astronaut Michael Collins gets into his space suit.

The goal of *Gemini 11* was to rendezvous with an Agena satellite on the first orbit around the earth. This would take split-second timing and exact control.

The spacecraft was launched September 12, with Navy Lieutenant Commander Richard F. Gordon and Pete Conrad. Their first-orbit rendezvous and docking with the Agena was successful.

Gordon was scheduled to take a long spacewalk. But like the astronauts before him, he had problems. Gordon's suit was so hot that his eyes were flooded with stinging sweat, blinding him at times. Finally he returned to the spacecraft, cutting his mission short.

After Gordon's walk, the Gemini crew fired up the thrusters and took the docked capsules to an altitude of 850 miles (1,368 kilometers). Conrad reported back to earth: "I'll tell you it's go up here, and the world's round." No human had ever flown so high above the earth.

Gemini 11 reentered the earth's atmosphere and landed 1.5 miles (2.4 kilometers) from its target. The astronauts had spent 71 hours, 17 minutes in outer space.

Above: Drifting toward a safe landing in the Atlantic Ocean, the *Gemini 11* spacecraft hangs from its main parachute on September 15, 1966.

LAST FLIGHT OF GEMINI

The final Gemini mission was launched on November 11, 1966. It was the fifth Gemini flight of the year. *Gemini 12* carried Air Force Major Edwin Aldrin and James Lovell. An Agena satellite was launched 90 minutes before Gemini.

Drawing on the spacewalking experiences of Cernan, Collins, and Gordon, Major Aldrin was better prepared for working in space. He had a pair of body harnesses that would secure him to either the Gemini or Agena capsules. A work area was fitted with foot holders to secure Aldrin while he worked with space tools.

Five hours after liftoff, the Gemini capsule successfully docked with the Agena. However, the Agena's thrusters had broken down after launch. The docked capsules could not fly to higher altitudes as planned. That left the spacewalk for Aldrin.

Aldrin was prepared. He spent 2 hours, 29 minutes walking in space.

He did not experience any of the problems that the other astronauts had. During the flight he made 3 separate spacewalks totaling 5 hours, 32 minutes. This had been the most successful spacewalk in human history.

Gemini 12 returned to earth 2.5 miles (4 kilometers) from its target. It was Project Gemini's last spaceflight. NASA claimed it as a success. The crew had rendezvoused and docked several times with the Agena. The 5-hour, 32-minute spacewalks set a record that would not fall for more than 10 years. All the tasks on the spacewalks had gone smoothly. There were no problems with exhaustion or overheating.

Project Gemini had triumphed—thanks to the bravery and skills of its pilots, and hard work of thousands of engineers and scientists. All of its goals were met. NASA was ready to move on to Project Apollo—putting a man on the moon.

Above: Astronaut Edwin Aldrin works outside the *Gemini 12* spacecraft on his record-breaking spacewalk.

Astronaut Ed White walking in space.

GLOSSARY

agency
A government bureau.

astronaut
A person trained for spaceflight. From the Latin words "star traveler."

atmosphere
The gaseous envelope surrounding the earth.

ballistic missile
A bomb that travels under its own power and guidance systems.

Cape Canaveral
A place on the Atlantic side of Florida where missiles and rockets are launched. Most missions into outer space were launched from here.

capsule
A small, pressurized area of a spacecraft.

Cold War
A period of strong rivalry between the Soviet Union and the United States that stopped just short of war. This period lasted from 1945 to 1991.

Communism
A system of government where most economic and social activity is controlled by the state.

cosmonaut
An astronaut who comes from the Soviet Union (Russia).

destroyer
A fast warship used as an escort in convoys.

engineer
A person who makes practical use of pure sciences such as physics and chemistry. Engineers use their scientific knowledge to build spacecraft.

launch
To send forth forcefully.

liberty
Freedom from bondage and outside control.

liftoff
The start of a rocket's flight from its launch pad, also called "blastoff."

media
Newspaper, magazine, book, radio, and television communications.

Mission Control
Ground control for spaceflights.

module
Any of the segments of a spacecraft designed for a specific task.

NASA
National Aeronautics and Space Administration. The government agency formed in 1958 to research and launch satellites and spacecraft.

nuclear
Involving atomic weapons.

orbit
The path of a satellite or spacecraft.

orbital
The area of an orbit in which a satellite or spacecraft flies.

rendezvous
A French word for meeting between two people or things.

retrorocket
A small rocket that slows down a spacecraft.

satellite
An object that orbits around a planet.

Soviet Union
A country of 15 republics in Eastern Europe that was ruled by a Communist government. Disbanded in 1991 and replaced by the Commonwealth of Independent States. Sometimes called Russia.

splashdown
The landing of a space vehicle in the ocean.

thruster
A rocket engine that steers a spacecraft.

Vostok
Name of the first manned spacecraft launched by the Soviet Union. Means "the East" in Russian, the official language of the Soviet Union.

warhead
The forward section of a missile that carries a bomb.

weightlessness
A state of floating experienced when in orbit. Weightlessness is caused by being out in space, far from the pull of the earth's gravity.

BIBLIOGRAPHY

Aldrin, Buzz. *Men From Earth*. New York: Bantam Books, 1989.

Arco Publishing. *Out of This World.* New York: Arco Publishing, 1985.

Dolan, Edward F. *Famous Firsts in Space*. New York: Cobblehill Books, 1989.

Gatland, Kenneth. *The Illustrated Encyclopedia of Space Technology*. New York: Orion Books, 1989.

Kennedy, Gregory P. *The First Men in Space*. New York: Chelsea House Publishers, 1991.

Olney, Ross Robert. *American in Space*. New York: Thomas Nelson, Inc., 1970.

Pogue, William R. *How Do You Go To The Bathroom In Space?* New York: Tom Doherty Books, 1985.

INDEX